THORNS AND ROSES

EDWARD AARON MUGABI

DEDICATION

For our dear sister
Tende Margaret Robina Ayanga of blessed memory

CONTENTS

EPIGRAPH

Thorns and roses grow on the same tree.
Kurdish Proverb

A roses rarest essence lives in the thorn.
Rumi

CHAPTER 1

Regina Wotali had forgotten to lower the message notification tone of her mobile phone, then its loud tinkle interrupted her moodiness. She lazily picked up her phone, checked inbox, half smiled. The incoming text message from her younger sister, Robina Namuwaya. *She is on the way here,* Regina thought.

She read the text. *Taron has travelled to Shenzhen. I am sorry I cannot come over today. I'll come sometime after his return.* The ghost of a smile that had graced her lips faded. She wondered if she should reply. She was in no state of mind to call or text back, mumbled something meaningless as the syllables of an unknown tongue.

Her sad and drowsy eyes squinted, then opened, watched the sun radiate its last light as it was gradually hiding behind the distant horizon. The silhouetted grey heron that was soaring in the sky, smiling at the earth, told her to be strong. She took a sip of water, sat quiet and cried. She cried until she tired and drifted into a vision, relived the past weeks.

She never took a test, her feminine intuition told her a baby was developing in her womb. She felt tiredness, faintness, morning sickness and a craving for pumpkins. She was the gladdest woman on earth, ecstatic, happy as a wave that dances on the sea. Whenever alone, she lullabied and caressed her stomach. She began a daily routine of taking selfies, created a photographic diary. She fantasised about naming her baby Olympia, never told her loving, ignorant husband, Howard Babyerabira.

A few weeks in development, she started experiencing minor cramping during the day when her husband was away. She felt concerned but wasn't alarmed. She reached for the guide she had hidden in her travel bag. She read it, was reassured many women felt sharp pains during pregnancy. A week later the cramps became like the dull ache that accompanies a heavy period. She felt pain throughout her womb and across her lower back. She didn't tell her husband, pretended it was period pains.

Midmorning the next Wednesday she started bleeding, losing brown blood. Fright gripped every cell in her body, her hand reached for the phone, dialled her husband.

'Where are you?'

'I am in the field.'

Howard, a community development officer with Mayuge district was conducting field work in his domicile sub county of Buwaaya. *She looked well this morning, why is she sounding tense, taut*, Howard wondered.

'Are you okay?' a disturbed Howard asked.

'I am bleeding, come take me to hospital.'

'Okay, please get ready.'

Howard rushed home, used his office's pickup truck.

As he stepped from the truck, Howard said, 'Wait, wait please,' to the driver. The driver, a slim tall young man named Zebulon Mbona, sat back and waited.

Upon entering the living room, Howard glanced around anxiously. He momentarily thought his wife was in the kitchen but walked to the master bedroom. Feelings of uneasiness, apprehension, dread, filled him.

His wife seemed exhausted, disoriented, confused and agitated. She was staring at him open-mouthed, with undried tears on her nose and cheek and a despairing look on her face.

Howard tried to hide his uneasiness but it seeped out, like the sweat visible on his brow. He stripped off his jacket, took a few deep breaths, calmed himself. *Lord God, save my wife*, he prayed. *Take her to hospital*, his brain screamed.

'Sir, good afternoon.' Howard had dialled his boss.

'Good afternoon. Are you in the field?' Malcom Onzi asked.

'No sir, I have left the field. My wife suddenly fell sick. I want to take her to hospital. I request permission to use the office vehicle to convey her.'

'It is alright. Please remind the driver to make entry in logbook and countersign.'

'I will. Thank you, sir.'

Regina felt dizzy, vaguely remembered her husband helped her change to clean clothes and then sat her in the back cabin. She had only a hazy recollection of the journey. They drove to Saint Francis Hospital Buluba at breakneck speed, jolted along the bumpy road. She nearly threw up at every bump they hit.

Given her condition and Howard's status of senior civil servant in the district she was booked in as "next patient to see doctor."

'For how long have you been bleeding?' Dr Anatolia Nabwire asked.

'I started bleeding this morning.'

Curiously, by the time she saw the doctor, the bleeding had stopped and her mind was clear. She explained the situation. As she explained the doctor kept interrupting her, asked her to repeat what she had just said. The doctor did that frequently, which was frustrating as it was disconcerting.

'I am admitting you. Your case needs detailed examination,' Dr Nabwire brusquely concluded.

Regina had never been hospitalised before, couldn't fathom if it was a necessary step. The part of her that wanted to know what was happening inside her however agreed to the admission.

Her husband escorted her to the maternity ward, a long building on the west lawn. The ward was full of pregnant women, she had never seen so many in one place. She was delighted the young and pretty admitting nurse secluded her, allocated her a curtained cubicle, albeit with a worn-out curtain.

Late in the afternoon she had an ultrasound scan and blood test to check her hormone levels. The technicians told her the doctor would give her the results.

After what felt like a day but was really one hour and a half, Dr Nabwire approached her in the ward and with the sensitivity that doctors lose over the years said, 'Your embryo has no heartbeat, you are having a miscarriage.'

Dr Nabwire kept talking but her words didn't register.

Dr Nabwire looked at Howard. He was standing by the bed, silent, watching her.

'I will give you two some privacy,' the doctor said.

Dr Nabwire must have sensed their fears. She put a reassuring arm on Regina. 'Don't be hard on yourself, this is not your fault. The loss roesn't mean that your next pregnancy will result in a miscarriage,' she said, then turned and left.

Howard's hand reached out for Regina's and she took it, even though she couldn't bring herself to look at him. A few minutes later, Howard released her hand and walked out. Later, he told her he didn't want her see him crying.

Oh, God, no! Regina sighed and leaned back on the pillow. Slow, salty tears spilled out of her dark brown eyes. She was disconsolate, couldn't believe her baby laid still in her womb, no longer a baby, a pregnancy loss.

'*Nga olabye inho inhabo.* Very sorry, so sorry madam,' echoed a chorus of voices throughout the ward. She was grateful for the limp curtain that separated her bed from other patients and their attendants. She never bothered to answer the sympathisers, stared dejectedly at the ceiling. *What did I do that may have caused this?* she thought to herself.

Having grown up perceiving hospitals to be beneficent places of caring and compassion, places to recover, she expected to be doted on. She would never forget that night. The cramping came with a vengeance, was very painful, she could hardly move her legs.

Disappointingly, the midwifes and nurses were cold-eyed, cranky, impatient, belittled her pain. Being in the maternity ward filled with pregnant women was additional torture for her, all she could hear was the cry of new born babies.

In the morning Dr Nabwire prescribed ibuprofen to ease the cramps.

The doctor returned a few hours later and examined her.

'You are likely to miscarry at any time. We will review you in a week. I will see you next Wednesday,' Dr Nabwire said, discharging her.

Regina glanced at her watch, noticed it was few minutes to two o'clock.

In spite of the fact that she was in pain she felt relieved to be discharged. Her mind leapt home, thought of comfort and privacy, appetising food, soft clean sheets and music that uplifts the soul. She had had enough of the cold curtained cubicle, the worryingly thin mattress and staff who were too cavalier in their treatment of patients.

She bid a half-hearted goodbye to the midwifes and nurses.

As she trudged to the exit, she kept saying to herself, *don't worry, the miscarriage will be over soon.* She imagined she would experience what seemed like a heavy period; a few hours of bleeding, clotting and cramping. She thought about the trip to Fort Portal she had put off when she reckoned that she was pregnant. She wished she had travelled.

***

On the drive home Regina was sullen. Her congenial smile, a smile that could buck up all who saw it, was gone, if it happened, inert.

The air of sadness and despondency around Regina made Howard hesitant, but then he decided he should ask. Her being secretive about the pregnancy had made him curious. He gave her a tender look, asked, 'Why did you not tell me you were pregnant?'

It is a question her mom Shelley K Babumba and mothers-in-law Zara Nangobi and Hawa Namusobya later asked when they came to commiserate them. Ma Zara was her father-in-law Levi Mugweri's first wife and Howard's mom, Ma Hawa was her co-wife.

She saw the look on her husband's face, knew he was hurting not only for the pregnancy loss, but for her as well. He was the one she depended on for strength and support, he needed comforting. Rearranging her face into a genial face, erasing the crestfallen one that had clung to her before, she said, 'I wasn't sure I was pregnant. My intention was to tell you after the first midwife appointment. I had scheduled it for next week.'

***

It was Howard who let the cat out of the bag, told Ma Zara, in turn she broke the news to the family. Her moms visited the very next morning and, as Howard was at work, spoke straight from the shoulder.

'Next time you get pregnant look for *akasandosando akatono* and *enkenge*, wavy leaf plant, squeeze their leaves in cold water, sieve and drink half a cup daily. It helps prevents miscarriage,' Ma Hawa said. 'If ever there is *musisi*, earthquake, when you are pregnant, tie a rope made out of *eikungu*, fibre from the *gheete* banana or *eikare*, banana leaves already used in cooking, around your waist. And in the last trimester rub skin which has sloughed off a snake on your belly. You will give birth with ease.'

Regina listened as if she had an exam for it. She jerked at mention of rubbing sloughed snake skin on belly. The mention took her to *terra incognita*, a totally unknown land.

'Lastly when you receive news of *okutwalana*, death of a woman during childbirth, pinch your ears and say "I have not heard that."

Ma Hawa liked being paid attention to. Everyone recognised she was knowledgeable about medicinal plants and rituals within minutes of meeting her, like it was her favourite badge by which to identify her. Every common ailment, she knew the herb, and if you disagreed with her, she wasn't angry, she just pitied you for being ignorant.

'Those herbs and rites are simple but effective,' her mom said.

Regina was surprised her mom agreed with Ma Hawa and concerned. Her mom had never spoken about the herbs and rituals before.

Then she noticed Ma Zara said nothing about the herbs and rituals.

'Nice *gomesi*.' Ma Zara complimented her mom.

'It's lovely, the flowers are pretty. Where did you buy it?' Ma Hawa asked.

Her mom's *gomesi*, floor length dress with square neckline and short puffed sleeves, worn with a sash tied in a bow-form around the waist, was a pastel shade of blue with beautiful imperial red roses.

'Thanks for the compliments. I bought it in Jinja. What about yours, where did you buy it?' her mom asked.

'I bought it in Iganga,' Ma Hawa said.

Ma Hawa's *gomesi* was striped triad of sapphire, midnight blue and indigo.

'Thank you for the care you extend to my daughter,' her mom said.

'You don't have to thank us, she is our daughter,' Ma Zara said.

'I understand. I am really grateful.' There was a brief silence before her mom continued. 'My in-laws, I admire your relationship.'

'*Bakazi banange*, my women friends, I learned long ago to be at peace. *Eisega mwoyo: tiriganha mukazi kweyaza.* If there is jealousy in a woman, she cannot have peace of mind,' Ma Zara said, citing a Lusoga proverb.

They all appreciated silently the wisdom shared by Ma Zara.

'I wonder how you cope with each other,' her mom enquired.

'We work together. Life is much easier when everyone cooperates,' Ma Hawa said. '*Obutaisania: bwayawula amatako.* Disagreement made the buttocks to separate.'

'*Ow'eighali awula omulogo, ghe bimuwaku aghaya.* A co-wife is better than a witch; when the jealousy is over, she chats,' Ma Zara said.

The moms glanced at each other. The laughter that followed was like the sudden outburst of the glad bird in the treetop.

Ma Zara leaned toward Regina and muttered to her, '*Otaghulira bubi mwana wange*, don't feel bad my daughter.'

She blushed, nodded in the affirmative.

Her moms hugged her goodbye at four o'clock.

'*Bukali musana*, it is still daytime,' her mom said.

'*Balamuse*! Greet them! *Lamusa inho baaba*, greet dad more,' Regina said.

'Do you want me to help you with anything?' Ma Zara asked.

'No.' Regina acted strong, did not let Ma Zara know she was feeling pain in her stomach.

***

The next two days were the most difficult of Regina's life. The pain she felt was the worst, she took double the prescribed dose of ibuprofen. She felt strong pain throughout her abdomen and lower back, the cramping intensified to the sensation of labour contractions. The bleeding exceeded what she had experienced in the past and she saw more clotting than usual.

After several hours of debilitating pain, she felt an upsurge of pressure come over her from her chest straight down to the pelvis. Her instinct alerted her there was an imminent evacuation. She ran to the latrine, felt something come out of her.

The following Monday she went back to hospital, two days earlier than her previously scheduled appointment, had an ultrasound scan. They confirmed what she had already detected, her precious gift from God was gone.

Also gone, was the image of watching her husband hold baby Olympia, the portrait of placing her baby in the crib, the picture of picking her up when she stumbled, the dream of teaching her to write her name. Many images she had conjured up were gone.

When she was told to take a test in ten days to confirm there were no pregnancy hormones left, her heart sunk. Her face collapsed as if it were a pricked balloon.

Returning home, lost in thought, she nearly fell off the *boda boda*, motorcycle taxi. She cursed loudly, disappointed by their lack of a family vehicle.

She bled slightly the next day and felt some cramping. *Heal me, O Lord, and I will be healed, Jeremiah 17:14*, she prayed. The fatigue, bloating and cravings went away mysteriously.

***

As dusk settled over the savanna it occurred to Regina that she should tell her uncle, Gustavus Guveera, lead overseer at Christ's Tabernacle Buwaaya, what had happened. She dialled, heard the familiar 'Jesus is Lord' caller tune and then her uncle's silvery voice.

'Hello Regina, good evening. I didn't see you last Sunday. Are you well? Is Howard fine?'

'Pastor, good evening. Howard is fine. Do you have a moment to talk?'

'Is there a problem?'

'Pastor, I had a miscarriage. Please pray for me.'

'Oh, no! *Mwana wange*, my daughter, *nga walabye inho enda okuvaamu*, I am very sorry about your miscarriage. It is painful what you are going through. Abide by the truth that God loves you, God is good all the time.'

'God is good all the time,' Regina repeated.

'God will see you through the difficult times. Place your confidence in His goodness. We know that for those who love God all things work together for good, Romans 8:28. God works all things for His glory and for our good.'

'Yes Pastor.'

'You may be having lots of questions. Those questions are not at all useful, stop worrying. Our God is a miracle worker. He can do anything, everything, things beyond our comprehension. His ways are not our ways, Isaiah 55:8-9. We don't know His ways or His thoughts. As Moses put it in Deuteronomy 29:29, "The secret things belong to the Lord our God, but the things that are revealed belong to us and our children forever, that we may do all the words of this law." We just have to believe in His promise.'

'Yes Pastor.'

She sensed the preacher in him had taken over, readied herself to note Scripture referenced.

'The Bible is the best book I know. It knows the human condition and experience well. God could have communicated with mankind in any way He pleased, and He chose the written word. Let Scripture set the text of your life. Don't give disappointment power. The Lord is close to the broken-hearted, Psalms 34:18. He comforts us in all our afflictions, 2 Corinthians 1:3-4. God will one day create a new heaven and a new earth. God's dwelling place will be among the people and He will dwell with them. He will wipe every tear from their eyes, there will be no more death or mourning or crying or pain for the old order of things would have passed away, Isaiah 65:17-25 and Revelation 21:1-5.' Pastor Guveera said, speaking to her as if from a script.

'Thanks Pastor, I will study the Scriptures.'

'Let us pray. God our Father, Father of mercies and God of all consolation, who throughout the ages has heard the cries of parents. We remember mothers and fathers whose babies died as a result of miscarriage, parents whose hearts are aching and arms are empty. We place Regina and Howard Babyerabira in your hands and we ask for healing, strength and love. Compassionate God, soothe them and give hope to their hearts. We pray in the name of Jesus Christ our Lord. Amen.'

'Amen.'

'You are in my prayers; I will continue praying for you. Do not fear to ask if you have unanswered or disturbing questions. I am available, just call me whenever you need me, where necessary we can arrange a meeting.'

'Thank you, Pastor.'

Good is good, gave us a Pastor who is a man of prayer, always on call, at all events seems to have the right words, loves sharing Scripture, Regina mused.

When she opened her WhatsApp an hour later, she was delighted to receive more Scripture from Pastor Guveera. "The steadfast love of the Lord never ceases; his mercies never come to an end, they are new every morning; great is your faithfulness," Lamentations 3:22-23.

She shared the telephone conversation with her husband, together they read Scripture and prayed. *Our Lord God, we are humbled and grieved. We were anticipating the birth of a child but the promise of a life was ended too soon. Our arms yearned to cradle a new life, our mouths to sing soft lullabies. Our hearts ache from the emptiness and silence. We are sad, we weep and mourn. Source of healing, we give you all our hurts, worries and cares. Make us strong in the face of what seems to be defeat, help us to find healing, restore our hope for children to come and give us courage in the days ahead. In the precious name of our loving Saviour Jesus Christ, we pray. Amen.*

***

The following afternoon, Regina received Mr and Mrs Kiwanuka, an elderly couple from the tabernacle, sent by Pastor Guveera.

'How is Howard?' Mrs Kiwanuka asked after the greetings.

'He is fine, he is at work,' Regina replied.

'I wish he was spending these days with you,' Mr Kiwanuka observed.

'There is no bereavement leave at his workplace, besides he is busy tidying up. He will soon travel for a workshop,' Regina said.

She served her guests African tea and fried liver.

'How are you feeling about your miscarriage?' Mrs Kiwanuka asked.

'It is a difficult situation to go through,' Regina said matter-of-factly.

'Our gracious Lord is our salvation in the time of trouble. Pray, ask him to be your arm every morning, Isaiah 33:2,' Mr Kiwanuka said.

They said a prayer, led by Mrs Kiwanuka.

'I very much appreciate that you came to see me, I will never forget it. Please give my regards to Pastor Guveera,' Regina said as her guests indicated they were about to leave.

Mrs Kiwanuka stood up and a warm smile lightened her face. She hugged Regina and said, 'Thank you for your gracious hospitality. I wish many blessings for you.'

'Thank you. God bless you,' Regina said.

'*Twidhie bulenga, twizeeyo bukere.* When we came, our stomachs were as thin as that of a frog and here we are going back with swollen stomachs as that of a toad. God be with you,' Mr Kiwanuka said, walking away, followed by his wife.

'God be with you too,' Regina said.

CHAPTER 2

'We are likely to receive a lot of visitors this week, I need help,' Regina said.

'I know,' Howard smiled. *Her exuberant personality attracts visitors.* For the first time he thought of his wife that way. That awareness reminded him of the saying, *omulungi ni mwanhina wabangi,* it is the beautiful one who is sister to many.

Another thought came to him, they lived a stone throw from his parents' home. Family and neighbours were likely to drop in. *Omusaayi gw'ow'ekika nkovu: teva ku mubiri.* A clansman's blood is like a scar; it never leaves the body. And *ow'omuliraano wa kika: bwafa tolima,* a neighbour is like a clansman; when one dies, you do not go to till the garden.

'You are just smiling, are you not doing something about it?'

'I spoke to the old lady. My younger sister Ayana Kyamwine is on school holiday, she will be with us the rest of her holiday.'

Regina smiled, 'Thanks for the arrangement.'

Howard left early for work the next morning.

After breakfast Regina, simply clad in Madagascar periwinkle *gomesi*, relaxed on the sofa. She was like that, always in clothes that understated her radiant beauty. Her ebony-black hair was cut short and her face was free of makeup. There was something about music that filled her, her feet were twitching to gospel playing in the background. It was a signal; her oxbow lips were ready to exercise charm over her guests.

A little while later there was a gentle knock at the door. She stood, walked to the door and opened it.

'*Tusangaire okubona*, you are welcome, glad to see you. How are you?'

'I am fine,' Ayana said bowing, ever demure and respectful.

'*Ali atya mama Zara*? How is Ma Zara?'

'She is fine.'

They greeted each other as they walked to the bedroom prepared for Ayana. Ayana placed her bag on the bed.

As they walked back to the living room Regina asked, 'How is school?'

'School is fine.'

'I hope you are performing well. *Ba mumalirivu oti maadhi ga mwiga: tigaira inhuma*. Be determined like the water of the river, it does not turn back.'

They were interrupted by a knock at the door.

Ayana walked to the door, opened it and welcomed her always cheery elder sister Agnes Tibaidhioghaya. She stepped back, motioned for her to enter first. Agnes gave her sister a sign that there was something on the veranda. Ayana looked, saw a banana bunch, two pineapples, one large pawpaw and polyethylene bag containing cow offals.

Smiling, Ayana called her sister-in-law, 'Agnes has brought food.'

'*Mulamu*, sister-in-law, welcome. *Weebale kwetwika*, thank you for what you have brought. *Otatoolanga okwo: Kibumba akwirizeegho gh'otoire*, never end at that, may God reward you, replace what you have given away,' Regina said, hugging Agnes.

They left the front door open, sat down.

'*Mulamu*, why did you not tell us?' Agnes asked.

At that moment, someone tapped at the door.

'*Koodi,* may I come in.'

'*Kalibu,* come in.'

'*Tusangaire okubona inhabo*, we are excited to see you madam,' Regina said.

'*Ninze asinze inhabo*, I am more excited to see you madam,' her co-sister Tiffany Biribonwa said.

The sisters greeted each other.

'I am so happy you have come to see me,' Regina said, sat next to Tiffany, admiring her knot of hair, a tight bun, not a strand out of place.

'*Isuusangaku omugongo*, well survived the backache. *Omuyini gumenheka embago yabaagho*, it is better the handle breaks rather than the hoe,' Tiffany said.

'True,' Agnes chirped in.

'You know I am a mother of four. *Mbakobele*! May I tell you! I had a miscarriage nine years ago. Miscarriage does not mean you are not going to be a mom,' Tiffany said.

Regina loved hearing that, breathed like a sea at rest. *Thank God, I am not the first in the family to have a miscarriage* was her first thought. The second, *don't give up, there is hope in the future. Bwe kitaligirya: eribika. Provided the mongoose does not eat the chicken, it will someday lay eggs.*

Again, there was a tap at the door. In walked a well-fed, courtly gentleman with a neat moustache, Lester Kaidhabwangu, Howard's friend and colleague at work. In his hands he carried a gift-wrapped box.

'*Tusangaire isebo*, you are welcome sir,' Regina said.

'*Zena nsangaire okubagaana bainhabo*, I am also delighted to find you home ladies. *Muli mutya bainhabo*? How are you ladies?' said Lester, sitting on sofa next to entrance, gingerly placing the box at his side.

'*Tuliyo balungi isebo*, we are well sir,' the ladies replied.

'*Weebale emirimo gyokola*, thanks for the work you do,' Regina said.

'*Kale*, okay.' Lester said.

'*Batya ab'ewuwo?* How are the people at your home?' Regina asked.

'*Baliyo balungi*, they are well,' Lester said.

'*Kirungi*, it is good,' Regina said.

'Mm…,' Lester said.

'Mm…,' Regina said, a note higher.

They sat in silence for a while until Lester said, '*Mukama waife antumye okuleta obubaka buno*, our boss sent me to deliver this message.'

Lester handed the gift box to Regina.

She unwrapped the present carefully, trying not to tear the paper, thereafter opened it. Her attention was arrested by an angel wing necklace in a beautiful keepsake case, a simple but elegant silver bracelet with the imprint "Too beautiful for earth," body butter, body scrub, essential oils and sympathy card conveying heartfelt message … we pray that all may go well with you and that you may be in good health, as it goes well with your soul, 3 John 1:2.

Delighted, Regina said, 'Sir, thank you very much.'

'You are welcome,' Lester said.

Regina turned to Ayana. 'Please make tea for our guest.'

'No tea please,' Lester said. 'I hope I am not asking too much. A glass of juice or water will do. I am in a hurry to get back to office. *Akubonaku akatono awula alagiriza*, a short visit is better than sending a message.'

Lester was served passion fruit juice and left a few minutes later.

Shortly afterwards Regina welcomed Howard's look alike, Job Dhamutuuba, her elder brother-in-law, Tiffany's husband.

'*Mulamu*, sister-in-law, *nga walaba inho*, I am so sorry,' Job said, giving Regina an envelope containing money.

A smile flashed over Regina's face, like sunshine over a flower.

'Brother,' meant it, regarded Job as the big brother she always wanted, felt he treated her like a sister. 'I am truly grateful from the bottom of my heart for this,' she said, patting the envelope. 'God bless you for your kind-heartedness.'

Further, she thanked Tiffany.

Job smiled.

'Let us prepare something for you to eat,' Regina said.

'*Weebale,* thanks, *ndilya olundi*, I will eat another day. Maybe a glass of water,' Job said.

Ayana served Job a glass of water.

After drinking the water, Job said, '*Tubonagane*, we will meet/see each other again soon.'

'*Kale isebo*, okay sir,' Regina said.

Job left with his wife Tiffany and sister Agnes.

Late in the afternoon, Regina welcomed fellow villagers, *Namwandu*, widow, Galaale and Mr and Mrs Bageyana, served them tea. She liked their talk, found it good-hearted, chatty, idiomatic as well.

Not long after *Namwandu* Galaale and the Bageyanas left, her husband walked in.

'*Isuukayo isebo*, welcome home sir,' Regina said.

'*Nviireyo inhabo*, I have returned madam.'

She waited until he was seated. 'How was your day?'

'Busy. My boss wants me to submit field work report and accountability before I travel for workshop. How was your day?'

She looked at him. 'I am sorry about the work pressure. We were kind of busy too, we received a lot of visitors. They cheered me up, brought us gifts.' She mentioned the visitors and gifts received. 'Promise you will contact them, thank them.'

'I sure will.' Howard knew the visitors meant a lot to his wife. They had comforted her, left a lasting impression.

For nearly a week Howard had felt like a failure, powerless and frustrated; the pregnancy loss had blindsided him, hit more than a blindside knockout punch. He hated that he had no control over what happened. He struggled with thoughts that he would be less of a man if in any way he expressed feelings of loss. He found it easier to throw himself into his work and just keep busy, that way assuage the feeling of grief and pain.

He wanted to be a dad so much, had always dreamed of children and the dad he would be. Comforted by the support of family and friends he figured it would be best to be at peace, more empathetic, pray, stay focused for each other and share gifts. He realised certain things can never be undone, one has to live with them. Time will help the healing process and with God's grace, they will have children someday.

The following day Howard phoned the visitors, thanked them.

***

Early Thursday morning, just after her husband left for work, Regina heard a motorcycle approach their house. She looked out the window, hurried out, smiling and enthusiastic, welcomed her dad, Jesse Babumba. They hugged each other.

She led him into the sitting room. Kneeling, she welcomed him again and greeted him. Ayana followed closely, knelt, greeted.

'*Mwana wange,* my daughter, *nga walaba inho enda okuvaamu,* I am very sorry about the miscarriage.'

She recognised how uncomfortable it must be for him to reconcile himself to her pregnancy loss, old men in her community usually did not communicate openly with their daughters about miscarriage.

'May I have a glass of water?' Pa Jesse asked.

Regina served him a glass of water.

They talked, caught up on life at home. She complimented her dad on his new ride, a Bajaj Boxer.

'Be not troubled or disheartened,' Pa Jesse inspirited his daughter. 'God has not forgotten you. You exist because He thought of you and gave you life. God is not unjust, remain hopeful. *Edhizaawula omughafu: Kibumba adhiwumba igulo irala.* That which saves a destitute, is already planned by God.'

Looking at her soft-spoken dad, Regina was reminded of his integrity, his altruism and diligence. She was proud of him, loved him dearly. In a life so ordinary he was extraordinary, a real-life superhero who turned a lowly beginning into success.

When she was seventeen, her dad told her, 'I stopped schooling when your granddad, Reuben Babumba, fell sick and died. I had just turned thirteen and it was hard times. Facing a grim future, I ended up joining the nearest meat kiosk, cutting meat, placing it on the shelf and wrapping it for customers. I was allowed to weigh after two years.'

Regina felt humbled.

'Those early efforts to sustain my mom and siblings were met with ridicule,' he told her.

Ten years later Pa Jesse opened a butcher shop in Immanhiro. The business grew over the next fifteen years to branches in Mayuge and Baitambogwe.

'Now they respect me. *Kibumba bw'akwidhukira eyakuseka talwa kukusekulula.* When God remembers you, the one who mocked you may end up admiring you.'

As a family, they were lucky, her dad's business catered for their sustenance and paid for their education.

'How is business?' Regina asked.

'Business is good, I am proceeding to Kaliro,' Pa Jesse said.

Previously unbeknownst to her, her dad sourced cattle directly from farmers in Busoga region and slaughtered them.

'*Baaba*, dad, *tuli kufumba eky'emisana*, we are cooking lunch,' Regina mildly protested.

'*Bukusuba: waayagana mukyalira wo*. You had better miss the food and meet the host,' Pa Jesse said, smiling. 'I met you, I have to go.'

Regina stood and saw him out.

'Well, I am off,' Pa Jesse said as he gave her a hearty hug in the driveway.

Smiling, Regina said, '*Ale baaba*, goodbye dad.'

Pa Jesse started the engine and moved. Regina said goodbye again and waved at him.

She watched till he was out of sight, then walked back into the house.

***

Two evenings later, walking to the latrine, Regina heard her teenage sisters-in-law by Ma Hawa make callous comments about her. Ma Hawa's house neighboured theirs and they shared latrine.

'I heard she wasn't pregnant, she faked it,' Joan Tibikunina said.

'True,' Nancy Nawudo giggled.

They muted their talk when they saw her.

Regina nearly uttered *disgusting* when she neared them, restrained herself. *What good would it do to exchange insults with these teenagers!*

She thought it strange, the two hadn't bothered visit or talk to her. She couldn't believe they were saying such things. A short time later she told her husband what she had heard.

Howard wasn't bowled over, grew up conscious of the silent division between his mom and Ma Hawa's siblings. Bitter feelings of resentment towards his siblings came up as he called to mind the proverb, *owa inhoko: awula owa lata wo*. A sibling with whom one shares a mother, is better than one with whom one shares a father.

'They have been saying that since you returned from hospital, that you did it to pressure me to buy a plot of land in Mayuge so we move to town.'

'W-what!' Regina exclaimed. 'Why didn't you tell me?'

'It is cruel, that is why I didn't tell you. Please do not confront them. *Ow'agabono agangi tomugema ku mutwe*, do not touch the head of a talkative person. Let sleeping dogs lie, let God be the judge. I am sure if it was one of their own line going through what you have gone through, they wouldn't be saying such things. Stay strong my dear.'

'Hmm, *oluya olunene: lukubonia bingi.* A big courtyard or family makes you see, hear a lot of things,' Regina whispered to herself.

CHAPTER 3

'*Wasuze otya inhabo*? How did you spend the night madam?' Zebulon said after Regina opened the front door.

'*Bulungi*, well,' Regina replied. '*Wasuze otya isebo?* How did you spend the night sir?'

'*Bulungi inhabo*, well madam.'

Regina stood on the porch, accepted delivery, a beautiful bouquet of red roses.

'I thought you had travelled with my husband.'

Zebulon saw her curiosity about his presence, explained, 'No madam, he travelled with the district planner. They used the planner's vehicle and driver.'

'When was this arrangement made?' Regina asked.

'He paid for the flowers before he left, three days ago, asked me to deliver them today.'

'*Weebale*, thank you,' Regina said, closing the door.

She made effort to call her husband to thank him for the roses, his phone was switched off. She placed the roses on the coffee table, sank into the sofa, recalled her first Valentine. Her handsome, Howard, stood tall, bright brown eyes, clean cut hair and full lips wearing a captivating smile that she had seen a handful of times. He handed her the sweetest romantic bouquet she had ever seen and said, 'I will always remember the day we met, the way you smiled at me, the way you made my heart melt. My love for you is like the warm steadfast sun, steadfast love I promise you.'

It was her first time to receive a bouquet of red roses. Already smitten, she was speechless, stood before him like a little statuesque figure.

He kissed her forehead, gently patted her back and whispered, 'I will love you till the end of time. Have I ever told you are beautiful?'

'No.'

'Your beauty bedazzles every sense in my body.'

She felt like her feet barely touched the ground.

Howard took her to an elegant restaurant in Jinja. She thought it fine, it was the first classy restaurant she had been to. The romantic dinner that followed was like a fairy-tale made real. He held the chair for her to sit. They sat at the back, private, relaxed, candle lit, red décor and marvellous music around them. She enjoyed her meal of sweet and sour vegetable soup, sautéed potatoes and grilled chicken garnished with steamed broccoli, sliced carrots al dente and French beans, chocolate and strawberry cake dessert, and her favourite drink, sweet red wine. She also tasted Amarula fruit cream liqueur.

She was happy throughout as Howard was jolly, held good conversation through the dinner and on the drive home.

Before she met him, she had imagined marrying someone from outside her cradle, a man who would take her to live in the city. Howard was her complete opposite on the matter, made her rethink her daydream.

'Mayuge is like a divine fingerprint, enchantingly rolling to the horizon like giant waves on a great ocean. My soul calls it the land of serenity, walking there brings a frisson of joy. In all the world it is the place where most days the sky is an expanse of dazzling blue, a sweet calm air infusing energy into our souls,' Howard said. 'It is a place of history and migration, home to a diverse population. It is where Bishop James

Hannington, the first martyr of the church in Uganda, died. It is the birthplace of Saint Matthias Mulumba.'

She had never thought of her birthplace that way.

'In Ntafugirwa you can never be sad or lonely, everywhere there is a smiling face or someone to chat with. The folks keep an eye out for each other and help out strangers. When something goes wrong the community comes together, rectifies the situation. Our community is resilient, hardworking and productive. Farmers arise at cockcrow to attend to their farms. We never lack food.'

She noticed Howard had a tendency to idealise his home but that was okay with her. She had nothing serious against village life, was worried about wacks in Bulyampindi that readied themselves as suitors. Then Mr and Mrs Basubagha, with a son in the smuggling business, had *kwekoba*, reported their interest to her parents.

Howard was the gentlest man she had ever met. He was so different from the guys at church where they first met and the boys who schooled with her at Bulyampindi nursery school, Magolofa Primary,

Kigandalo Secondary and Iganga Teacher Training College. He never asked to sleep with her before marriage despite the chances they had. There was something of the spirit of a warrior, the heart of a lion combined with nobility and the soul of an angel that made her feel this was a gentleman she could love for eternity. Her soul had found its home. He was the ideal man she had dreamt of. And he was fine-boned, smart, humble, family-oriented, matured and optimistic.

She leaned back in the sofa, holding the bouquet in her hand. Her husband was not around to show her affection, she felt lonely. She looked at the thorns on the stem and thought, *how can a beautiful flower spring from a plant that harbours many thorns?* She took a stem out of the bouquet, got a painful rebuke. A big, mean, vicious thorn had slashed her wrist. All at once she hated the bouquet, wanted to thrash it but couldn't bring herself to destroy something that symbolised love for her.

She stared at the source of her pain, wondered whether it was a bouquet of thorns or a bouquet of roses. A sudden awareness came to her ... she was staring at her life. Her life was a bouquet of thorns. She just had a miscarriage. *What is there to celebrate about Valentine's Day?* she questioned herself. The joy of the event drained out and she gave off antipathies as a liquid gives off vapour. She felt bitterness towards her husband, he didn't appear sad enough after the miscarriage, showed no hurt. She was irked, he didn't take leave from work, moved on quickly. Worse he had travelled to Arua, over 570 kilometres away, to attend three weeks' community development workshop while she was in recovery.

Then her only sister Robina, whose visit she coveted since Ayana returned to school, had sent a text message saying she could not come over.

That night she ground her teeth. She woke up with a sore jaw, neck ache and headache. The soreness continued into the next day. Within three days she was having a constant headache, especially in the temples. *What is happening to me?* She googled, learned she was experiencing bruxism, that one of the leading causes are elevated levels of emotional stress and anxiety. *How do you explain it! How does emotional stress manifest in the jaw!* she wondered.

Sometime afterwards she realised she was holding back unexpressed thoughts, emotions and beliefs she had since childhood. The held back were coming out as nervousness and grinding of teeth during sleep. As a child and young adult, she had believed her adult life would be a flawless sequence of marriage, children and happiness. When she got pregnant, she dreamt of life with Olympia, her would-be firstborn, what they would do, where they would go, the schools she would study in, what adventures they would share, but the simple truth she had failed. She hated her body for what felt like betrayal, humiliation. She doubted whether it would cooperate the way nature intended, that is to say, grow, nurture and produce baby.

Instinctively she opened her 'mom-to-be' album on her mobile phone and looked at the pictures she took during pregnancy. The photos awoke a fond of herself, helped her to be kinder and less judgemental of herself. They made her recognise the positive that she got to be pregnant, experienced its elation, sensations and changes. That familiar phrase *forgive yourself* echoed in her ears. Something about the simplicity of that statement arrested her attention, made her curious and woke her out of the daze. After that the teeth grinding lessened and went away eventually.

***

The room was dark, outside was quiet you could have literally heard a pin drop. No *bodas* riding by, honking their horns. The nearby village bar, video shack and sports betting shop were closed, all customers were probably asleep in their beds except the night dancers. Even the crickets were quiet, their high-pitched chirps silenced, perchance drowsing.

Regina lay on their queen-sized bed. Even though she was in her comfort zone she could not sleep. Her mind was clouded with thoughts about the mean telephone conversation she had with her mom that evening. She remembered it all, replayed it.

'Mom, thanks for visiting me.'

'You are welcome.'

'How is dad?'

'I left him fine.'

'Mom, where are you?'

'I am in Jinja, visiting your sister.'

'How long have you been there?'

'Three days.'

'You visited me one day but have spent three days at Robina's place.' Regina spoke with firmness in her voice.

'Don't be selfish, get over it.'

By all odds Regina knew, her directness would be met with anger and it was.

'I can't believe this! I guess you are the reason Robina didn't come over.'

'You are always finding fault with me,' her mom said with an adolescent defensiveness.

'When is she coming over?'

'I don't know. I am planning to return home next week.' With her mom, Robina took precedence.

'May I talk to her?'

'She has gone to the supermarket.'

'I see …' Regina paused, briefly appeared to be at a loss for words.

Her voice turned serious. 'Mom, whenever I talk to you these days you get annoyed with me, why?'

'You know why! You, you, you … it is always about you. You have always been difficult, constantly wanted to be the centre of attention.' Her mom repeated a mantra she had bestowed upon her throughout her childhood.

She remembered her youth. The more she protested the mantra, the more she confirmed, lived up to the reputation of being difficult.

'You will never change your perception of me.'

'It is you who will never change, that is why you married that damned toiler.'

Her mom esteemed Taron, a well-heeled entrepreneur cohabiting with Robina. Howard was not moneyed, hence her derogatory remarks about his work.

'Till when will you stop referring to my husband as a toiler? He holds an officer position.'

'I wonder what kind of children you will produce, how you will look after them, possibly Providence arranged a miscarriage to save you from hurt.'

Once more, she was at a loss for words. *What on God's Earth had happened to mom!*

Her mom, hang up.

When she put the phone down, she was trembling. The fact that it was her mom's voice that sounded so full of acrimony was hard to bear.

She remained in shock for several minutes. Waves of anxiety and anger tore through her. She cried, tried to imagine what made her mom say those words. *What made her think it was okay to say what she said when it was not okay*? Fragments of critical moments in her childhood, teen years, college and beyond flashed through her mind. Again, and again, the tale, *Oh, yes! That happened because I was mom's least favourite!*

That night she realised her position as least favourite daughter was etched in stone. She feared the favouritism would never end. Her mom was likely to carry it on to the next generation. Saddened by these thoughts she remembered the words of the Buddha,

"Holding on to anger is like grasping hot coal with the intent of throwing it at someone else, you are the one getting burned."

Fear not; you are more valuable than many sparrows, Matthew 10:29, Luke 12:7, Regina comforted herself. *Lord, I know you are working on my prayers for children. I vow that when I am a mom someday, I will never show favouritism to my children. It is so hurtful. I understand if you show 'favouritism,' 'partiality,' 'respect of other persons,' 'servile regard,' 'snobbery,' you are committing sin, James 2:9.*

She became thoughtful and prayerful. Thoughts of favouritism in the Bible, Cain and Abel, Isaac and Ishmael, Jacob and Esau, Joseph and his brothers, came to her.

If you do well, you will be appreciated, but if you do not do well, sin crouches at the door and it desires you, but you must rule over it, Genesis 4:6-7 - thus the Lord spoke unto Cain that he may bring him to repentance and knowledge of his sin. Holy Spirit, reveal to me areas of my life where I repeatedly disappoint you.

Help me to overcome all temptation, so I may have victory over evil.

Favouritism was not the culprit in the case of Cain whose name signified possession. He was of that wicked one, his own works were evil, 1 John 3:12.

Abel signified breath, vapour, vanity and that is what he became to Eve. And that is what the things of this world are 'like the wind,' 'like vapour,' 'vanity, vanity, vanity,' temporary and transitory. Lord thank you for the gift of life, especially my new life in Jesus Christ. We are afflicted in every way but not crushed, perplexed but no driven to despair, persecuted but not forsaken, struck down but not destroyed, 2 Corinthians 4:8.

Abel expressed humility, sincerity, gratefulness and believing obedience. By faith he offered unto God a more excellent sacrifice than Cain, by which he obtained witness that he was righteous, God testifying of his gifts: and through his faith, though he died, he still speaks, Hebrews 11:4. God notices all our sinful passions and disappointments. Let not sin therefore reign in your mortal body, to make you obey its passions, Romans 6:12. Lord, may I strive to present myself as a living sacrifice, doing all things with honour and excellence, as you deserve my very best effort.

Regina recognised there was preference of the second born over the elder in Isaac and Jacob. There was suffering of the one passed over, not only in Cain's wandering, but in Ishmael's banishment, Esau's cry and Joseph's abandonment. Contrasting the jealous and murderous Cain with the tale of Joseph, she realised Joseph and his brothers reconciled so their descendants united themselves as the people of Israel. *So then pursue things which make for peace and things wherewith one may edify another, Romans 14:19. For the sake of your future children do everything in your power to maintain your relationship with your mom,* echoed in her consciousness.

She accepted her mom for who she was, believed this was a situation to deal with and learn from. She remembered the pain of bruxism, feared to stress herself again. She thought it best to forgive, stop muddying her present with thoughts of resentment and hurt.

Mom, I forgive you, Regina silently said. *I haven't forgotten what you said, you hurt me but I have managed to forgive you. Maybe you want to know why, it is because I love you. And I know you love me.* She felt better for it, forgave herself for taking so long to get rid of the excess baggage.

Perhaps this is maturity, Regina thought. That thought seemed to have led her discover that forgiveness is a complex process. *The reward of forgiveness is,* quoting her favourite from Cheryl Strayed, *"you've found a way forward that acknowledges harm done and hurt caused without letting either your anger or pain rule your life or define your relationship with the one who did you wrong." The downer is that you are never actually finished. It is ultimately about the disposed. No matter who wronged, the disposed is still the bigger debtor, has to forgive, from the heart "seventy times seven," Matthew 18:22.* She realised we don't forgive for others sake, we forgive for our own.

God, please forgive and bless my mom, she prayed.

Her mom called her in the morning.

'I feel terrible about last night. I was wrong to say what I said.'

'You are right mom. You were so hard on me.'

'I know I hurt your feelings. I was unfair, mean and insensitive. I am sorry.'

'There is no need to apologise mom. I forgave you.'

CHAPTER 4

'Long time, how are you?' Regina said.

Nashmia Tiberowoza, an old girlfriend from Kigandalo Secondary, and a born of Bulyampindi was on the line.

'I am well, could be better,' Nashmia said.

'You sound low spirited.'

'I had a miscarriage four days ago.'

'I am so sorry. This is going to sound crazy. I also had a miscarriage.'

'I am very sorry,' Nashmia said. 'Before, I thought miscarriages were uncommon.'

'I reckon they happen often. I also think there are many untold stories of miscarriage we never get to know because we, women, rarely talk about it.'

'You are right. Until recently I had no idea my mom had two miscarriages.'

Regina hesitated, wondered whether to tell Nashmia about her co-sister Tiffany's reveal that she had a miscarriage nine years ago. Thankfully Nashmia changed the subject.

'Do you hope to be in Jinja soon? If you do, please give me a call, let us have a meal together.'

'Okay dear.'

'Hey, congratulations for your sister. I met her in the supermarket last week. She told me she is pregnant.'

Regina was silent.

'Are you still on the line?' Nashmia asked.

'Yes. I was thinking about our upcoming family get-together,' Regina lied.

'Has she told you about the pregnancy?'

'Of course, she told me,' Regina lied again.

After she hang up the phone, Regina took a deep breath. So many thoughts and emotions rushed through her. She worked it out, her mom was visiting Robina; she was aware of the pregnancy.

Regina loved her sister, was happy for her, however it pained her that they had concealed pregnancy news from her. *They acted unreasonable, unkind and in way that could damage their sisterhood. They should have been more sensitive, called or come over*, she reasoned.

Or maybe it was all her fault, created by karma she built when she didn't tell the family about her pregnancy.

She was undecided whether to call Robina and congratulate her or keep quiet till they told her.

***

The days that followed were a blur of events.

It was a little white cat that started the whole thing. As Regina sat eating dinner she looked up, saw a tiny white cat hanging by a loop from the lightbulb. She watched with eyes that could not believe, the cat dissolved like some unsubstantial vision faded. Somewhere in the neighbourhood a cat meowed and a dog barked.

She felt weird, couldn't sleep because she kept thinking about a real baby Olympia falling and crashing into the latrine. The vision was vivid, it was like a memory. She felt guilt, sobbed for hours, then fell asleep.

She awoke to the sound of a baby crying. There are no words for how she felt. Her heart sank right through her skin onto the bed she had slept on. She looked around the bedroom where she felt she was not alone, hummed a lullaby.

She stayed in bed all-day, drinking black tea, eating bread and roast groundnuts. She didn't want to discuss her matters with anyone, didn't want anyone to disturb her, at least wanted a sign that read 'do not disturb' around her.

She stared at her phone for a long time and then dialled her husband. 'You lied that you travelled for workshop. I know you are on a different mission.' That is all she said, hang up.

Howard was confused and upset. He thought the conversation strange, made mental note to speak to her about it later.

The following morning, she felt lonesome, somehow talked herself into visiting her dad. In a stupor, like someone under hypnosis, she walked out of the house, unusually slowly, almost robotically. She got lost, was without her mobile phone. Eventually it was her uncle

Will Tirubuza who recognised her sitting under a roadside mango tree in neighbourhood of Bugwanandala that took her to Bulyampindi.

Pa Jesse was baffled, had never seen his daughter in such a fogged state, she could easily have passed off as walking zombie. Twilight had fallen. He didn't know what to do at that time, told self to be patient, take her to hospital in the morning.

He dialled his son-in-law. His phone was switched off. He dialled his wife who was still visiting Robina. Next, he dialled Howard's mom. He told them Regina was found lost. Not to worry them, he told them she was stable, sleeping.

Ma Zara reached Howard at night-time.

'When are you coming back?'

Howard noticed her voice was worried.

'I am travelling, should be home tomorrow.'

'Okay, I called to inform your wife is not well.'

The news gave Howard lots of questions. He recalled his wife's accusation that he lied about workshop, realised it was undisputable, something was wrong.

Regina was so lost in her mind she was not aware her dad was struggling. He was bearing all responsibility around the house, directing the maid to arrange her bedroom, give her food and bath water.

Pa Jesse spent the night by his daughter's bedside, worried that if he left something bad could happen to her. He prayed all night for her health and wellbeing.

***

'How, when did it start?' Lester asked. With concerns over Regina's health, he had rushed to Howard's home after learning of his return.

'*Muna*, my friend, *bino bikusobera*, it is puzzling,' Howard replied.

'*Kusobera oti kirevu ekirekerera ente ni kigema embuzi*, quite puzzling like a beard which grows on a he-goat other than a bull.'

'Yes.'

'I think your wife was bewitched.'

'No, I don't think so.'

'*Kabwidhdibwidhi n'omwana ow'omulogo*, very clever like the child of a witch. Be clever and take action.'

'Lester, you need deliverance. The things you are talking about are an abomination to the Lord, Leviticus 19:26, Deuteronomy 18:10-12.'

'I am telling you! You should visit *omuyigha*, healer, not *omulaguzi*, fortune teller, *omusawo w'ekinansi*, traditional doctor, *omusamize*, one who gets possessed, or *omuswezi*, traditional priest.'

'They are all the same, besides *okulagulwa kunia obulogo*. To seek a fortune teller leads to practising witchcraft. Diviners usually associate client's problems with their respective families, neighbours or friends as the causes.'

'*Lubaale, mbera nga n'embiro kwotaire*, God helps those who help themselves. I say you should visit *omuyigha*,' insisted Lester.

'I have a kind request. Will you accompany me to Bulyampindi?'

'Yes, I will.' Lester was Howard's groomsman five years ago. He thought it his responsibility to accompany his friend to his in-laws.

It sounded as though there was a knock at the door. Howard hurried to answer, welcomed Ma Hawa.

They greeted her.

'I am sorry about your wife's health. I think she is suffering *amakiro*, mental illness that attacks a woman after childbirth. Get *amaadhi ag'omunkompe*, water from the hole of a tree, and use it to wash her head,' Ma Hawa said.

Howard gave Lester a bewildered look as he wondered why Ma Zara said nothing about *amakiro* when he spoke to her earlier. He thanked Ma Hawa, a hint of doubt in his voice and then he and Lester left for Bulyampindi.

***

Regina woke up fresh as a jewel found but yesterday. Amazingly, she had no recollection whatsoever of what happened in the past few days, simply wanted to return to her marital home.

Pa Jesse was surprised everything appeared normal. While he wondered what mystery had happened, he was delighted his daughter had come back to herself. He was thankful for the miracle of recovery, said a prayer of gratitude.

When Regina went to the dining room for breakfast, her dad was already at the table.

She picked up her mug of tea just as the maid rushed in. 'Madam and Robina have arrived,' Layla Kyaliki said.

A look of surprise briefly reflected on Regina's face. She wasn't sure how to act.

Then Robina walked in. She wasn't a girl anymore and she would never be again. She had just entered that noticeably pregnant stage, her waist was beginning to expand. She was dressed in modish cotton dress of pink magnolia. Her face was made up, but not overdone and her hair was braided. Her pretty lips were carefully tinted red and her cheeks had a subtle rosy glow.

Smiling inwardly, Regina recalled four or five events where two distant relatives thought she was Robina. People often made the mistake especially when she wore a *gomesi* and they looked at her from a distance. True, there was some likeness between them.

She had missed her sister. She and Robina were born six years apart, so growing up were at different stages. She was required to babysit, watch her at home and school, teach her chores. There were inevitable squabbles between them as Robina liked to 'borrow' her clothes, books and accessories including rings, bracelets and handkerchiefs.

Their dad was little involved in disciplining them. He was at work most of the time, absent from home except on Sundays. Mom was the task master and disciplinarian. She had a quiver of arrows, all crafted to chasten her, Regina, and not Robina. Her mom faulted her, yelled at her, contended she was supposed to know better than her younger sister, accused her of being difficult and seeking attention, sometimes looked on, did nothing. Somehow, they survived those sensitive years. She didn't know it then but the way she mentored Robina they bonded, forged a close relationship.

Regina looked at her sister again, caught on to what was going on. Her resentment of her mom's favouritism had triggered her nerves, made her envy her sister's pregnancy.

Truth be told, her mom had always considered her the difficult one and Robina was the favoured, golden child. She did when they were younger, still did in adulthood. She was thankful she and Robina recognised the annoying favouritism, were friends. The thought reminded her of lesson learned through the years that family love is unconditional; friends come and go, but family is forever. Our sibling relationships, in fact, are the longest lasting family ties we have.

Regina observed some shyness about Robina that morning, as if she was feeling contrite about something. They hugged.

'Because of what you have just been through, I wanted to tell you in person that you are going to be an aunt. I was coming over next week. I didn't want mom to be the one to tell you,' Robina said as she cast a glance at her mom who had followed her in.

Her mom hugged her. 'She wanted to be the one to give you the news. Believe me, I am not protecting her.'

Regina kept her head down and made sure not to upset her mom. She had turned her hurt to God, was satisfied with the action she took, it was not necessary to bicker back and forth about why neither of them gave her the pregnancy news earlier.

Regina turned to Robina. 'Don't worry about me, congratulations dear. God bless you with a happy, healthy pregnancy.'

The sisters retreated to their bedroom.

'Solidarity! Why did you not tell me about the pregnancy?' Robina asked.

'My apologies. I wanted to surprise you, announce it on my birthday.'

Robina warmly smiled at her and Regina smiled back.

Regina was relieved, not the relief of knowing Robina accepted her apology, but the relief of knowing she understood her quirks.

'Trust me, I was thinking about you all the time,' Robina said.

Regina understood, Robina was afraid of hurting their relationship.

Marriage had distanced their relationship; they rarely saw each other nowadays. It was time to catch up with her only sister, her lifelong friend, the yin to her yang, her loyal supporter and cheerleader.

They talked about the miscarriage, shared tips on absolutely everything from how to deal with the heartburn and constipation, how to dress the baby bump and the best brand of diapers on the market, gossiped about celebs and cracked jokes. It turned out to be comforting and healing, allowed Regina to let go all rankle on her mind.

'*Kikoiko*, here is a riddle,' Robina unexpectedly said. She said it with a sentimental voice and a sappy grin, an arrangement they adopted as kids when they wanted to play *bikoiko*, riddles.

'*Kiidhe*, let it come,' Regina said, laughing.

'*Ndi ni mukazi wange bw'agya ewaibwe aira nga ali mabunda*. I have a wife but whenever she goes to her parent's home, she comes back pregnant.'

'*Ensuwa*, a pot.' A pot is made out of clay and water but when it is taken to the well, it comes back with water.

Robina smiled smugly. 'Here is another riddle.'

Always observing, Regina saw the smile of satisfaction on Robina's face. 'Let it come.'

'*Omukazi muka mukagwa wange mpa lulimi lw'atoogera*. There is no language my friend's wife doesn't speak.'

'*Laadiyo*, radio,' Regina roared.

Flinging back their heads, the sisters laughed and laughed.

By the time Howard and Lester arrived everything was happy, it was loving all around.

Howard had imagined he would find an indisposed Regina, had wondered how he would react. He felt an overwhelming sense of relief that she was well and his in-laws were relaxed and cordial. The good mood continued throughout the visit and it was a pleasant trip back home.

CHAPTER 5

The multicoloured, artfully arranged bouquet was delivered by a courier, a wiry *boda* man in a hurry. As soon as Regina opened the door he thrust it into her arms, turned sharply and left.

The flowers were enchanting lavender, fascinating orange, modest peach, and innocent white roses. A smile grew on her face as she touched the lavender and whites with her fingertips. They were cooler than she expected, smoother too.

Her phone rang.

'Have they delivered the flowers?' Howard asked.

'Yes, they have. I love them, thank you.' *Why the attraction, was she receiving psychometric healing?* Regina reflected.

'Nice to know, see you in the evening.' *Thank God she was herself again.* Howard was relieved she was out of what he assumed was a fugue state.

Soon Regina placed the bouquet in a vase, poured water. *I ought to have roses every day. I need to buy preservative to add to the water,* she assessed. *Aunt Rosaline Bimuli, a floriculturist, has grown roses for a decade on farm in Bufulubi. I should visit her one of these days, learn growing roses.*

As she sat admiring the roses, she recalled the ancient Roman legend of many suitors that were lined up to marry a beautiful woman named Rodanthe, but she had little interest in any of them. The men were so full of love and desire for her that they became rowdy and eventually broke down the doors to her house. The incident angered the goddess Diana who turned the woman into a flower and her suitors into thorns to teach them a lesson. She chuckled at the memory.

Up out of the blue she had a flashback to the day a thorn pierced her. *Why do we always thank God for the roses, never thank Him for the thorns?*

A few moments later, comprehension unknotted in her brows. *The rose is what it is because of the thorns. Thorns protect the rose, harm only those who would steal the blossom.* She felt shame. *Jesus wore a crown of thorns, an emblem of his love for us, a vicarious testimony that he bore both the evil of our sins following rebellion in the garden of Eden and the curse we received, so that we might one day wear the crown of life and glory, 1 Peter 5:4, Revelation 2:10.*

Tears rolled down her cheeks.

It was a real epiphany for her. She recalled Scripture, "give thanks in all circumstances; for this is the will of God in Christ Jesus for you," 1 Thessalonians 5:18, appreciated God is working beyond the circumstances. The good and bad times are important for we grow through both. She remembered Pastor Guveera once telling her that pain, thorns and brambles, are everywhere. They are hidden in everything we see and touch. Every bunch of roses is a beautiful thorn necklace. Everyone has one and as Rumi say, a roses rarest essence lives in the thorns.

Penitent, she dropped to her knees, bowed her head and prayed. *Heavenly Father, thank you for being with us through the difficult times. Help us to see the blessings in the hard times and help us to be faithful to serve You no matter what circumstances we face. Your grace is sufficient, for Your power is made perfect in weakness, 2 Corinthians 12:7-10. Lead us to walk by faith and pray breakthroughs. I choose to have faith in Your ability to break through every obstacle in my life. In You we boast all the day long and praise Your name forever, Psalm 44:8. My life is a journey and I am so grateful that You are on it with me. I know Your plans for me are wonderful and perfectly timed. I will triumph in You. In Jesus' mighty name I pray. Amen.*

She also prayed that she sows not among thorns, Jeremiah 4:3, Mark 4:3-20 nor reap thorns, Jeremiah 12:13, Hebrews 6:7-8. Further she prayed for faith to grow in her motherland. When we let God's word accomplish its purpose in us, instead of the thorn shall come up the noble cypress, instead of briar shall come up the myrtle: and it shall make a name for the Lord, an everlasting sign that shall not be cut off, Isaiah 55:11-13.

***

An hour after talking to his wife, Howard received a call from his dad that Joan was sick at her boarding school.

'Please go see her. If she is very sick and needs to be taken to a hospital for proper care, please come back with her. We will take her to the hospital,' Pa Levi said.

Zebulon drove Howard to Wekolele High School.

The school stood on a broad ridge and looked over a spread of sugarcane fields and swampland. It was about forty years old. Pleasingly its students performed well in the O and A levels.

The offices, classrooms, library and science laboratories were rows of buildings gazing at the north entrance gate. Behind them lay a large playground slanting gently towards the O level dormitories and staff houses on the south side. Sprouting eucalyptus trees covered the east side.

Mrs Bettina Omoit, the head teacher, a picture of contentment, a person in a profession she loved, welcomed Howard. She was tall and shapely; her hair was greying and her eyes spoke of a nurturing soul.

'Thank for trusting us with your daughter's education.'

'She is my sister,' Howard broke in.

'Oh, yes!' Somewhat surprisingly, Mrs Omoit was not embarrassed by her gaffe. She continued with an expressionless face. 'Joan does not sleep, has poor concentration in class and doesn't complete coursework. She has complained about the teachers, that they are not helping her.'

'How long has this been going on?' Howard asked.

'A fortnight. The school nurse has done her best, kept Joan at the school clinic in the second week. In her opinion Joan has prolonged sadness, insomnia and forgetfulness. She recommends you take her to a medical facility to establish what is causing these complications.'

'May I talk to the nurse?' Howard turned his eyes to the nurse. 'Why is Joan having prolonged sadness?'

Mrs Omoit glanced at Nurse Ritza Tibaghulawo who had listened while sitting po-faced, like she was lost to worrying thoughts. When she turned to speak, Nurse Ritza softened her face and said, 'Joan is awake all day, doesn't sleep at night. Last night I gave her a sleeping pill. She slept a while, hallucinated, screamed and jumped out of bed. She said she saw tall, black crouching creatures with eyes as white as white satin hissing at her and walking towards her bed.'

W-what! Has she received any other medication?' Howard asked.

'No,' Nurse Ritza said.

'Where is she?' Howard asked.

'She is at the clinic,' Nurse Ritza said.

They walked to the clinic which stood alone, next to the A level dormitory, not far from the dining hall and chapel and looked over swampland in the west. It was clean and the air had an undertone of bleach. It was as comfortable as a classroom.

Joan was the only patient. She lay on her back, her head rested on a pillow. She had an expressionless face, was emaciated and her hair was uncombed.

'Has she not been eating?' Howard asked.

'She does not like food, stares at her meals the way she stares at the ceiling when she should be sleeping,' Nurse Ritza said.

'How are you feeling?' Howard gently asked.

'I can't explain it, but I am not feeling alright,' Joan said in a low voice.

'Joan needs medical treatment, I am taking her,' Howard said decisively.

Joan was very emotional on the way. She cried and repeatedly said, 'I need to protect my mom.'

Halfway towards home they sighted a man with blackened face, tatty shirt and threadbare trousers, carrying loads of dirty plastic bags, rummaging the roadside trash. Quite unexpectedly Joan stopped crying, quieted.

By the time they got home, night had fallen and enveloped the sky in a blanket of darkness. *Eibonamulala*, a shooting star, zoomed past. It brought to Howard's mind the youth days. Whenever he saw it, he wished upon it, asked for something he desired before if disappeared. '*Oyo lubaale kyaka*, that is the god that lightens,' his granddad Nehemiah Kafuko had told him. 'Whoever sees it is a lucky person. Always make a wish when you see it.'

Howard walked to the front door holding Joan's hand. The porch light was on and the ubiquitous daylight bulb supplied by Umeme, the electricity distribution company, cast a glow on the veranda. He knocked. The door opened slowly, and Morgan Dhabangi, his youngest brother's face was revealed. Grinning, Morgan opened the door wide and they entered.

Pa Levi was seated in the living room, in his favourite spot, *mwami akooye*, a recliner, his and his only. He was watching football on the television.

Howard said greeting and sat down.

'Dad, the school administrators say Joan has insomnia, melancholy and forgetfulness.'

Pa Levi, an elderly gentleman with a fringe of smoky-grey hair around his balding scalp, watched his daughter, waited for her to say greeting. Independent and casual, relaxed and slow to anger, analysing situations with ease, Pa Levi noticed his daughter was reluctant to greet him. He greeted her, 'How are you?'

Joan didn't answer, instead ranted unintelligible babble about heaven, hell, angels and *badhaadha*, the ancestral spirits. She wandered around the living room with her arms stretched out as if on the cross. She called, 'Messiah, Messiah, Messiah! Oh yes, heaven is a place on Earth. I am going to build God's tabernacle here in Ntafugirwa.'

'This is not my daughter, there is something wrong with her,' Pa Levi said, low.

Howard was silent, but agreed.

Ma Hawa walked in, sat next to Joan.

Joan stared at her mom, her brown eyes near black and gleaming with relentless intensity, leaned over and whispered in a different voice from hers, '*Badhaadha* have asked me to protect you.'

Ma Hawa felt fear, as though a chill wind was blowing through her body.

Afterwards Joan started laughing uncontrollably, said, 'I have grand plans for the universe. I am going to make Mayuge the capital of the world.'

A sigh of anxiety leapt out of Ma Hawa's mouth.

Surprised by her blathering, Pa Levi turned, said to Howard, 'Tomorrow take her to Butabika.'

Ma Hawa held Joan's hand and said, 'My daughter is not insane. I will not allow you to take her to Butabika psychiatric hospital.' In Ma Hawa's thoughts

Joan needed sleep, was probably anxious about the imminent O level examinations.

In the maelstrom Ma Hawa stood and walked Joan to her house.

As they left Pa Levi said to Ma Hawa, 'Please don't leave Joan by herself, stay close to her. She looks weak, feed her well.'

The forlorn look in his old man's eyes, Howard would never forget. 'I wanted to be anyone else in this world so I could wipe the sadness from dad's downcast face,' Howard later told Regina.

***

Joan skipped dinner. She said she had no appetite. She drank tea and retreated to her room.

Ma Hawa tried to sleep but it was next to impossible. It was hard, so hard for her to accept Joan's bizarre behaviour. All night her mind regurgitated the evening.

The morning was no exception.

'Did you sleep well?' Ma Hawa asked

'Mom, I am scared to sleep,' Joan said.

'Why?'

Joan didn't answer, didn't explain that weird things happened to her. Every time she closed her eyes, she saw strange creatures.

A few hours later Joan heard unusual voices in her head commanding her to sing. The voices were totally different from her thoughts. She whispered Jesus Christ over and over, but the voices continued, gradually became louder, intense and repetitive. Unknown lyrics came to her. Her mom told her later she sang a disjointed version of *Kanambeya*.

Kanambeya ono, Kanambeya akalezi ak'obwende
Bamulungira ku lugyo
Kanambeya oyo, bingi bye yamugha
Kanambeya oyo, kanambeya oyo
Mutoolere obwala, muteeku n'engoma
Kanambeya oyo, yamufumba bwire, tibamufumba misana
Kanambeya ono, bamulunga mu kyayi
Ghakulema mu kyayi, omuteera mu iva
Kanambeya oyo bamuteera mu safuta

Ghakulema mu safuta, omusimba mu bigere

Kanambeya oyo, bamuteera mu bulili

Kanambeya oyo, bingi bye yampa

Kanambeya ono, Namusobya agolola

Kanambeya ono, olwemba nsiibwire

Translated

The herb *kanambeya*, the little love charm

It is cooked on a potsherd

That *kanambeya* gave her many things

That *kanambeya*, that *kanambeya*

Start clapping and beat the drums

That *kanambeya*, she cooked it at night, they don't
cook it during day

This *kanambeya*, is cooked in tea

If he defeats you in tea, put it in his sauce

That *kanambeya*, they put it in his bike's shaft

If it does not work in the shaft, you plant it his
footmark

That *kanambeya*, they put it in his bed

That *kanambeya* gave her many things

This *kanambeya*, Namusobya is going

This *kanambeya*, I take leave of this song

Joan sang for about an hour. Exhausted, she fell asleep in an instant.

Listening to her daughter singing Ma Hawa realised the matter at hand was her problem to shoulder. She became panic-stricken, anxious tears trickled down her cheeks.

Throughout the day she pondered what herbs to administer to Joan, was desperate for a solution. At nightfall she reached conclusion she did not have enough information about the condition, matter required consultations.

The following day she visited a confidant not far from their residence.

'*Nsangaire okukubona inhabo*, I am excited to see you madam, 'Daisy Edhirumamwino said.

'*Kale, ninze asinze*, thank you, I am more excited to see you,' Ma Hawa replied.

'*Osibye otya inhabo*? How was your day?'

'*Bulungi inhabo*, well madam.'

'*Ombuzeeku!* It's been long since we talked. *Obanga gha*? Where have you been?'

'*Mbaileyo eka*, I have been at home. *Tuli balwaire*, we are sick.'

'*Muli balwaire*? You are sick?'

'*Muwala wange Tibikunina mulwaire*, my daughter Tibikunina is sick.' Ma Hawa liked to refer to Joan by her surname.

'*Alwaire ki*? What is she suffering from? *Musuudha*? Fever?'

'*Mbe ti musuudha*, no it's not fever. *Tibikunina alokompoka*, Tibikunina babbles incoherent and meaningless things, *akoba nti badhaadha bamutuma okunkuma*, says the ancestral spirits have asked her to protect me.'

'*Ekyo ekizibu kinene!* That is a big problem! *Wetaaga okubona omufumu*, you need to see a diviner who reveals,' Daisy said. 'I suggest you see Saddam Wamukota. He is the best I know and he never disappoints.'

'Where is his workplace? Is it far from here?'

'He lives and works in Jirijiri, Nsango parish.'

'Ooh, he resides in Buwaaya.'

'Yes. By *boda* it takes about half an hour to reach his place.'

'I should leave very early.'

'You should, he is always busy, receives a lot of patients. *Kambasabire*, I am praying for you'

'*Weebale era tusabire inho*, thanks and pray a lot for us.'

CHAPTER 6

The night was long, the hours crawled by like years. Ma Hawa slept fitfully and awoke before the roosters crowed, unable to rest with her troubled thoughts. She had asked her brother Yaqub Godyo who owned a motorcycle to transport her. She had told him she was going to do something important, that she didn't want to involve her husband family.

By dawns early light Yaqub arrived from Makoova township where he lived.

'We better hurry,' Ma Hawa said as she sat on the carrier. 'I don't want family and neighbours to see us leaving.'

'Where are we going?' Yaqub asked.

'We are going to Jirijiri to see *omufumu* Saddam Wamukota.'

'Why are you visiting a diviner?'

'*Azira naku tayawukira ya isabo*, the one without a problem does not go to a shrine.'

Ma Hawa filled him in on Joan's condition as they rode.

Yaqub was quiet. It seemed something was bothering him, maybe he was offended his sister had not revealed her 'important' matter earlier.

On the way they passed farmers going to their gardens, carrying hoes on their shoulders. They saw school children walking by the roadside.

They passed an eatery shack that had opened for business. It served a choice of tea or coffee and *katogo*, a boiled mixture of cassava and beans, to its earliest customers.

They neared their destination, left the loose gravel road and followed a dirt track lined with trees and shrubs. After riding past a sugarcane plantation, they reached their destination.

There was no hint of dawn, the yolk looking sun had turned from remote yellow to golden and its gentle heat could be felt. The azure sea overhead showed no signs of rain. It was the perfect day for a visit.

They parked in the front yard, surprisingly it was newly swept. There were three Toyota Ipsum, two

Subaru Forester, a Nissan Jeep, a Mitsubishi Pajero, an old Mercedes Benz, seven motorcycles and a tired bicycle. It was clear the owners were also visiting the diviner.

The diviner's residence was a burnt brick house with corrugated iron roofing. A kit of pigeons strutted along the roof, cooing rhythmically. A faint smile escaped Ma Hawa despite her cloudy mood. She interpreted the cooing as a welcome.

A few paces to her right a whirlwind started. It was like welcoming her, dust flew past her. She closed her eyes to keep the dust from getting into them. Straight ahead was a lush banana grove, coffee, cocoa, moringa and jackfruit trees. The banana leaves rustled, twigs were hurled, even the mulch flew as the wind passed through the grove. It vanished in the corridor separating the bananas from the coffee.

An usher who had been watching her since she dismounted the motorcycle directed her to the shrine, a large round grass thatched hut of wattle and mud, in the backyard. In its inner surroundings, *akawuna, oluzibantaawo, olufaafa, akasibante, olweto* and *katatyamusulo* shrub-like plants were grown. She knew the herbs were protection of the shrine against evil forces, brought good luck, in addition were used in treatment.

She found a queue, joined it. Most of the patients were women and young children.

Four goats were tethered nearby, one pawed the ground with her forelegs and bleated softly. She wasn't surprised to see goats close to the shrine. She was aware goats were at times required as payment, occasionally were offered for immolation or ritual.

Hard to miss was a slender, dark-complexioned middle-aged lady dressed in coral patterned with straight and curved rosewood lines *gomesi*. She stood a few metres away, watched silently. Ma Hawa guessed she was the goat owner, was watching her goats and position in queue.

Thirty minutes later the 'goat lady' entered the shrine. Surprisingly she came out after five minutes and her face was smiles. As she walked across the compound and left, Ma Hawa wondered, *were the goats a return, thanks to the diviner?*

People were coming in numbers you could swear they had been invited for a community or social event. The numbers confirmed Daisy's remark, the *mufumu* received a lot of patients.

'We made the right decision, coming early,' said the plump woman next to her.

Ma Hawa did not respond to the talk.

An hour went by and another. Like a player biding her time to serve as a substitute, Ma Hawa waited patiently.

Eventually her turn came, she walked in.

The shrine was dimly-lit and reeking of incense. The diviner sat on bark cloth atop mat on the floor. He was nothing like she had imagined him to be. She had visualised him to be an old man with a wizened face. She saw a fitter looking man, with an athletic body and barely looked like he was over thirty. He was respectably dressed in crisp beige shirt, a sleeveless waistcoat made of bark cloth and khaki trousers.

There was calmness about him. He smiled, introduced himself. She half-expected he would fall into a trance, instead he sat quietly like he was listening to something then looked at her and said, 'Your family is in trouble. With the help of someone like me you took *omukyeno*, haunting spirit, to your home. It might make you daughter crazy.'

Ma Hawa had never been so confused. Trepidation swelled through her as she raised her eyes to read the diviner's inscrutable face.

'Do you remember!' His voice was calm, drawled.

Ma Hawa shifted uncomfortably on the mat.

Silence lingered in the air. Ma Hawa's head buzzed with possibilities, reconstructing scenarios that could have brought the evil. She mulled over them for a while, laboriously recalled the events.

Three years ago, she visited *omusawo w'ekinansi*, witchdoctor, named Bruce Kaisokampanga, long since dead. Then that practice was next to her birthplace in Bulyaiyobyo, Bugiri district.

'Our daughter-in-law Regina Wotali has made me suffer. Ever since she came, my son no longer looks after me. I don't care if she gets mad, fails to conceive or if she conceives gets a miscarriage,' Ma Hawa said.

'I can do all that,' Kaisokampanga replied.

Ma Hawa believed him. 'That is what I want.'

'Are you sure?' asked a sober faced Kaisokampanga.

'Yes. We will get our son another wife who will serve me well,' Ma Hawa said.

Kaisokampanga put twelve *ensimbi endaguzi*, cowrie shells, in his right hand, shook them and threw them on the knackered bark cloth before him.

'You are going to triumph,' Kaisokampanga said, pointing at a cowrie that stood atop another.

Ma Hawa was elated at interpretation that the cowries predicted victory.

The *musawo* forthwith prepared a mixture, handed her *ekibya*, clay dish, sized dose and half litre bottle of water. She was not aware that the mixture was largely soil taken from grave of person who suffered insanity and that water was collected from a turbulent spot in Lake Victoria.

As instructed, Ma Hawa bought *enkoko ensesere*, chicken with raised feathers, slaughtered it, let the blood drop on the 'medicine' at the same time cursed Regina. Afterward she buried the items in a dead anthill.

'Does your son not take care of you?' Saddam asked.

The question brought Ma Hawa back to the present. 'He does take care of me,' she answered.

'Does your daughter not treat you well?'

'She treats me well.'

'*Byewakola nebilibalondoola*, what you did is haunting your family.' Saddam's expression was serious but not unkind.

Byewakola ..., what you did is haunting ...! The words kept reverberating in her ears like the tolling of a bell. Panic, rage, shame and fear raced through her as she realised what the words meant; evil, resulting from her visit to Kaisokampanga, stayed at their home. Her stomach knotted up and she almost bit her tongue into two.

Saddam looked at her haunted face. It was rigid with tension and fear, she seemed to have aged a decade in the past few minutes.

'Ma, why did you misuse the anthill? Don't you know that homeless spirits reside in anthills?'

Ma Hawa stared at him. There was a glazed hue to her eyes that made the diviner think she was losing her marbles.

'Don't worry, your daughter will get well. I will capture the *mukyeno*. In the meantime, you have to withdraw the curse you put on your daughter-in-law.'

'How do I withdraw the curse?' Every nerve in her body seemed like a strained harp-string near breaking point.

'Do not cause trouble again. Remember, *Lubaale ow'ekiswa: tasonkwamu lwala*. The Lubaale spirit of an anthill cannot be poked with a finger. Go back to the anthill, call all spirits from the east and west, and of your clan, withdraw your curse. After recanting, bless your daughter-in-law that you wrongly accused.'

Ma Hawa watched the *mufumu* but appeared not to. The only thing she was aware of was her heart hammering against her rib cage. She was awestruck by the diviner's ability to read her. It was spooky he knew what she did.

The equipment of his trade and medicine were neatly stacked against the wall. With a single hand, Saddam picked a blue plastic tin, opened it.

'Later, give your daughter this treatment.'

The *mufumu* gave her six seeds of the *basaadhabakirana* flower, told her to pound and mix the paste with a cup of milk, then give her daughter a quarter cup once a day for some time.

He told her to pay the equivalent of twenty-one dollars. Ma Hawa placed the money in the small decorated basket before her.

'You know what to do. You must withdraw the curse, only then will the medicine work. You don't have to visit me again. I will capture and bury the *mukyeno* tonight.'

Strange, Ma Hawa thought. *He doesn't sound like a diviner looking to maximise profits from me as a client.*

Ma Hawa walked out of the shrine, squinting at the bright sunshine. She was on the verge of tears. Yaqub approached, gave her a hug, she welcomed it.

'He prescribed a paste of flower seeds, gave me six seeds,' Ma Hawa told Yaqub.

They rode home silently.

Ma Hawa thanked Yaqub, requested him to drop her a short distance off. She walked the remainder of the way home.

***

Joan preferred to be alone, isolating herself in her room, like she wanted to be in quiet settings.

Returning from the *mufumu*, Ma Hawa found Joan seated on her bed, dazed as a sea disturbed by opposing winds, babbling on about *badhaadha*. In a deep man's voice, Joan mentioned *Wunhi, Mukama, Mukasa, Kiwanuka, Muwanga, Bunha, Budhagaali, Waitambogwe, Lukoghe, Isegya, Mutabula, Kawumpuli, Kifaalu, Nakalanga, Namugaba, Nambaga, Kasanakampoomera* and *Basaadha* repeatedly.

Ma Hawa's heart rate ascended. She could feel her pulse pounding in the temples.

Days later Joan told her mom that she was frightened like a toddler in the dark. She revealed she saw faces of people she had never met streaming before her eyes and heard mocking voices as she mentioned *badhaadha*.

Before Ma Hawa knew it, Joan levitated above the bed, shouted, 'To reclaim your soul, return to the hill.'

A minute later, Joan descended onto the bed. She had a weird grin.

Again, Ma Hawa filled with jitters, her heart pounded faster. She worried her daughter was possessed by evil spirits.

Umpteen times remorse etched at her heart. Guilt gnawed at her conscience, her head felt like it was hollowed out and swarmed with maggots. Hot, shameful tears trickled down her cheeks.

What-ifs flooded her mind. For hours she contemplated the worst. She didn't know how she was going to handle Joan if her condition worsened. Utmost, she didn't how she would cope with the pain of knowing her actions caused the trouble. She wished for a Time Turner so she could go back, rectify the wrong. She wished her misstep would drain away, like the rain, go away.

Remorseful. Guilty. That is how she felt in quiet moments, such as when she was going to sleep or squatting in the latrine. She envied the walls of her bedroom, hard and lifeless, unable to feel the torments of life.

In time it became clear she had the option to do what the *mufumu* advised.

The following Saturday evening, Ma Hawa went back to the anthill where cursing took place, called upon the spirits, added, '*Ndhiza omunwa: mwana wange Regina Wotali, nhendha kukugha obwibuka, ofune eidembe, neisanhu, ba mulamu.* I withdraw my words. My daughter Regina Wotali, I want to bless you so that you receive godsends, peace and happiness, be healthy.'

CHAPTER 7

It was a sunlit day of late April and the sky was brilliant blue. As expected, Regina found her aunt in the backyard.

'Aunt, you look tired,' Regina remarked.

'Work, my dear,' Aunt Rosaline said, pointed to the trench she had dug that morning. 'It has been raining a lot lately. Roses need a soil that drains well but holds onto moisture long enough so the roots absorb some more.'

'I see you have already made today's delivery. What time did you wake up?'

'I wake up at first cockcrow, early morning is the best time to pluck roses. After we have arranged them, a van collects and distributes them to florists in Jinja and Iganga.'

'How many workers do you have?'

'I have four gardeners who help with plucking. If I employ more, will I make a profit?

Regina didn't answer, only smiled.

'That field,' Aunt Rosaline pointed to the adjacent two acres. 'We spend two hours plucking it. Let's go.'

Regina followed her aunt around the boundaries. *Roses have thorns, unlike your aunt you have no protective wear. Be careful.* Her aunt was wearing a loose-fitting ochre dress, a sleevelet, sturdy gloves and gumboots.

'I only use organic manure, cow dung and coffee husks,' Aunt Rosaline explained.

The garden was quite a spectacle, looked like a massive carpet of flowers. It blazed with tidy rows of white, yellow, orange, red and lavender roses waving in the breeze like a smile born of the cosmos. Regina paused, admired their brilliant shades, sensed their aroma, let herself be in the moment with their transient beauty. She looked up, saw a weaverbird swoop across the field to its nearby nest, smiled. *That bird is lucky, has a spectacular view of the roses.*

'Roses have been around for a long time. so long that they have powerful symbolic value in many cultures and traditions. Nowadays people associate the roses, especially the red ones, with love and romance,'

Aunt Rosaline said. 'The rose is the sweetest thing God ever made. All elements of the rose are valuable, can be used for healing purposes.'

Regina looked at her aunt the way an archaeology rookie might look at a professor describing recently discovered artifacts of a quaint and lost world.

'That is interesting.'

'Yes, it is interesting.' Aunt Rosaline said, looking at Regina lovingly. 'Did you know roses can be prepared as teas, jellies, sauces, seasonings, syrups, tinctures, wine, pellets or capsules? They can also be prepared as healing crystals, creams and lotions, as incenses and oils that are used in making perfumes and fragrances.'

'I didn't know. What a lovely thing a rose is!' Regina said.

When they got back to the house, her aunt prepared an orchard-fresh bouquet and gave it to her.

'Thank you so much aunt,' Regina said, deeply grateful for the bouquet and learning about growing roses.

She kept the bouquet for a week, remembered her aunt and smiled whenever she glanced at it. That week she realised she felt happier, was less anxious, calm and had a healthy natural sleep. Even her husband appeared more relaxed.

So clear, thanks to recent experience and the mellowing hand of time, there was something about flowers that helps our health and wellbeing. Kazuko Okakura was right, "In joy or sadness, flowers are our constant friends." The thought made her smile.

Being a mythology geek, she read literature on flowers. She was over the moon about roses when she learned that in Greek mythology, Melampus, the great seer, used the Christmas rose as herb to cure the madness of Proetus' daughters and other Greek women, who lost their hair and roamed wildly through mountains and desert of Tiryns, thinking themselves to be cows. Her excitement about the fact that Mother Nature is a healer and one of the most powerful gifts comes in the form of flowers, led her resolve to be a rose farmer.

'Why do you want to grow roses?' Howard asked when she communicated her resolution.

'You know roses bloom on Aunt Rosaline's farm. And so far, she thrives as a rose farmer.'

Howard was silent.

Regina worried, her husband appeared disinterested.

'Roses are rich in vitamin C.'

Howard looked at her. 'Can they, as other C vitamins, help fight flus, colds, allergies and be used in skin care?'

A modest smile crossed Regina's lips. 'Yes, and more! The petals can be eaten raw to increase blood circulation, they also relieve anxiety and depression as the rose possesses mildly laxative properties.'

'That means they can help in serious conditions like heart disease and stroke.'

'Yes,' Regina said smiling.

There was a moment of silence.

'This is the most enthused you have ever been about roses. I am praying you succeed in your endeavour. Let your hope make you glad.' Howard admired her determination and was happy she had taken time to study the growing of roses.

Regina was delighted they agreed on growing roses. Howard had discouraged her from her field of teaching. She had been posted, first to Nakibungulya Primary School in Kamuli district, then to Saint Francis Budini Girls in Kaliro district. He said the schools were far, and wanted her home as a housewife.

With a wide smile and eyes full of hope Regina said, 'Thank you sweetheart.'

***

'I am going to be honest with you,' Ma Hawa said.

It was her opening gambit. She had finally gathered the courage to unburden her guilty heart. She was tired of thinking about what she held was Kaisokampanga's treachery and wickedness. For the first time in her life, she knew she needed to ask for forgiveness for wrongs she had done.

Howard and Regina said nothing.

'All of us who have lived a certain amount of life, have a few things to regret. Some things we wish we had done or not done. Some things gnaw at us at the wee hours of a sleepless night and make us wonder, what if I had done or not done that! This is such a story.' Ma Hawa paused.

Howard and Regina continued to be silent.

'Three years ago, I visited a witchdoctor. After the visit I did things, I regret I shouldn't have done as they caused Regina's miscarriage and Tibikunina's sickness. My dear children, what I did was wrong. I feel badly that it caused you hurt. I am deeply ashamed of my actions. I ask you to forgive me,'

Ma Hawa didn't tell them that she had given up visiting witchdoctors, that after forty days she planned to say ruqyah seeking refuge in Allah from the evils of her actions, that she planned to read Soorat al-Baqarah for forty days. She kept the Muslim faith when she entered into a customary marriage with Pa Levi, allowed her children to practise their father's faith.

Heavyhearted, Howard slouched into his chair. *It is a shame that a person we take care of turned her back on us*. The thought pierced him like a thorn. *The demon-beast of sin has subtly persisted, if it is not consciously stopped it might become a way of life as prophesied in Jeremiah 4:22, "For my people are foolish, they have not known me, they are stupid children, and they have no understanding, they are wise to do evil, but to do good they have no knowledge." O Lord, let the wickedness of the wicked come to an end; but establish the just: for the righteous God trieth the hearts and reins, Psalms 7:9.*

'I know you probably hate me now and I don't blame you. I can't apologise enough. I am sorry for everything I did. I am sorry I caused you pain,' Ma Hawa said, a touch of nervousness in her voice.

Regina sat still, close to tears. Ma Hawa's demeanour perturbed her. It was the first time she had seen Ma Hawa so ill at ease. She surmised visit to witchdoctor happened.

Again, she turned her eyes on Ma Hawa. The tortured look in Ma Hawa's eyes told her conjecture was right. It was clear, for three years, her second mother-in-law, who she treated as her own, had an evil secret. *But why, why did she do what she did?* Naught came to her thoughts.

She recalled a witticism Nashmia said years ago, 'If you want a happy marriage, find a mother-in-law from hell!' She had told Nashmia she wouldn't pursue that. Paradoxically she had found one!

As a person she abhorred conflict, always wanted to be a daughter-in-law who got along with her extended family. A strained relationship where Ma Hawa and her children avoided her seemed a possibility at that point in time.

A week ago, she had noticed Ma Hawa was not her usual conversationalist self. Ma Hawa had become a reclusive neighbour, hurriedly retreated into her house after greetings, refused to answer inquiries about Joan's health. She didn't think much of it at the time.

Right at that moment she understood what had been going on in her neighbourhood!

She felt empathy towards Ma Hawa, saw her as a 'victim' of the culture that shaped her. She saw that the Ma Hawa seated before them had internalised her problems, realised that what she did was wrong, was hurting and seeking forgiveness. There was no mistaking what had to be done.

What Ma Hawa said she did was something she would remember all her life, Regina thought over. *Imagine the humiliation of apologising to your children. Ma Hawa faced, suffered it. Forwards it was best to forgive, walk by the Spirit, abide in Jesus, receive peace and control against sinful things.*

She looked at her husband, saw the hurt in his eyes. She silently spoke to him, *Fret not yourself because of evildoers, neither be envious against the workers of iniquity, Psalms 37.*

Before she could whisper to her husband, *Mama is seeking our forgiveness,* Howard said to Ma Hawa, 'You are our mom.'

From that moment on she realised her husband's thoughts completed hers on the matter.

'The Bible instructs us to let all bitterness, wrath, anger, clamour, slander, along with malice be put away from us. Instead, we should be kind to one another, tender-hearted, forgiving one another, as God in Christ forgave us, Ephesians 4:31-32,' Howard said.

'True, we are to love,' Regina said. 'Jesus said "love your enemies, do good to those who hate you, bless those who curse you, pray for those who despitefully use you," Matthew 5:44 and Luke 6:27-28.'

Regina gestured to her husband, he stood. They walked over, knelt, placed hands on Ma Hawa's shoulders. Regina was silent for a moment, then prayed. *Merciful Lord, thank you for the gift of forgiveness. We pray that you bestow it upon us your family. Bless Ma Hawa, protect her, help her find peace. Lord, have mercy on Joan Tibikunina, come to her aid. Help us to keep in step with your Holy Spirit and be counselled by your word. Help us to set our minds on things that are above, not on things that are on earth, Colossians 3:2. We ask for your patience as you work your will, show us how to be loving Christians that you have called us to be. We pray in Jesus' name. Amen.*

Ma Hawa felt like a dreadful burden had been lifted off her shoulders.

'My dear children,' Ma Hawa said, touching the shoulders of Howard and Regina, still kneeling beside her. 'I want our family to be happy and I will do whatever it takes to assure that. I bless you. May you receive peace and happiness, stay healthy, fertile and bring forth *empanga n'ensenhe,* boys and girls.'

Teary eyed, the couple said, almost in unison, 'Amen. Thank you, mom.'

Ma Hawa had carried a bottle of water. She drank from it and blew it over Regina first, then Howard, as a blessing. Thereafter she gave them the remainder to drink.

That night Regina started a prayer against witchcraft. *In the name of Jesus Christ, our Lord and Saviour, I bind all principalities, powers of the air, rulers of darkness, spiritual forces of evil in high places and I forbid them to operate against us; spirits from the netherworld, spirits between, over and around those praying and those prayed for and all discarnate, familiar spirits are completely bound and forbidden to manifest; I bind and break witchcraft; I bind and break the power of all curses spoken, all rituals or sacrifices, all divination, spells, incantations, all sorcery or magic, wicked rooms and evil hands. Lord bless those who are being cursed and those who are blindly cursing them. Arise and embarrass me with miracles and testimonies in the name of Jesus. I release and call upon the Spirit of the Lord, the spirit of wisdom and understanding, the spirit of counsel and might, the spirit of knowledge and the fear of the Lord, Isaiah 11:2. Thank you Father that no weapon the enemy forms against us shall prosper, because we are covered by the blood of Jesus and You have put all things under His feet, Isaiah 54:17, Ephesians 1:22. Because Christ dwells in us, we declare that greater is He that is in us than he who is in the world, 1 John 4:4. Amen.*

***

'Our ancestors were right. *Gw'olya n'aye n'akulyamu olukwe*, the one with whom you eat, is the one who betrays you,' Howard said.

They were out of office having lunch. The restaurant in which they sat was on the eastern flank of the newly built town council building. Its cuisine was steamed and boiled, no fried food. It was a restaurant for the elite of Mayuge, as well as their guests. Furniture was imported from China. Their table could sit four but it was the two of them that occupied it, diagonally across from each other.

'Why do you speak so?' Lester asked, curious and uneasy, wondering what accusations his friend had against him.

Barely looking up from his plate Howard said, 'People put their trust in sorcery rather than God and end up creating problems for themselves and others.'

'Why are you speaking proverbially today?' a tensed Lester asked, wondering what Howard was about to say next.

'*Ateesiga Kibumba ni kalaani w'abalogo*, the one who does not trust God is the secretary of the witches.'

'There you go again,' Lester said resignedly.

'Ma Hawa contrived to bewitch my wife, apparently Joan's sickness originated from her actions,' Howard said.

'You refused to accept when I suggested your wife was bewitched, how did you find out?'

'*Kyotaabona buto: okibona obukulu*. What you did not see when young, you may see in old age. I couldn't believe it, Ma Hawa confessed.'

'Some people do wrong and pretend not to know what is happening,' Lester said. 'My suspicion that your wife was bewitched heightened when Ma Hawa said Regina was suffering *amakiro. Amangudhungudhu ag'omulogo: gayimba okwita n'okwebuuzisa.* The so-called wisdom of a witch, it combines killing and asking for information.'

All the while Howard was thinking about something his parents prayed should not happen to him. "Levelling," the wicked habit of using witchcraft to pull others down. In his thoughts, *a people develop when they lift each other, not when they ruin.*

'It is unfortunate! *Omulamu: tayenda ya mwine ekube ibiri.* A human being does not wish his friend's domesticated animal to produce twins.'

Lester chuckled at Howard's darkening face.

'The only certainties in life may be death, taxes and the presence of wicked people,' Howard said. Death, taxes and wicked people are inevitable in this world we live in. It was his favourite maxim, learned it from his dad.

'You are right. Judas Iscariot dipped his hand with Jesus in the dish, the same betrayed him,' Lester said. 'People pretend to be what they are not. *Abalamu nswa, y'ebwika ku ngulu nga munda mwereere.* People are like the white ant, it covers itself outside, but inside it is naked.'

Howard sipped his water, looked at his watch and said, 'I can't believe it is already two o'clock. Let's settle bill and get back to office.'

***

Three weeks after her confession Ma Hawa visited Regina, gave her a big motherly hug, said, 'My dear daughter, I love you.'

Regina was somewhat surprised, Ma Hawa had never said 'I love you' to her before.

On the other hand, her conscience was clear. Unforgiving people are hateful, angry and bitter. Hate, anger and bitterness were toxic emotions. She had collected them, put them in a box called peeves and poured them in the drainage. She had chosen the path of

Christian love; love your neighbour, love your enemies, show them kindness and respect.

'Mom, thank you. I love you back.'

She wished Ma Hawa was a Christian. She would have given her Scripture she meditated regularly on. *Trust God to protect you from your enemies, Psalms 55-59. Always, overcome evil with good, Romans 12:21. God wants us to do good works, Ephesians 2:10, sees even when we give a cup of water to someone in need, Matthew 10:42. He blesses us when we bless others, curses those who curse us, Genesis 12:3.*

Ma Hawa was in a relaxed and confident mood. There was none of the embarrassed and agonised look about her that she displayed on the day she confessed.

'With your conduct you gave me a splendid lesson in humility and morality, may God abundantly bless you.'

'Amen.'

A radiant look came over Ma Hawa's face, like a sudden burst of sunshine on a cloudy day. 'Tibikunina is well. She is going back to school tomorrow.'

'Praise the Lord.' *God had not only touched Ma Hawa's heart, He had healed Joan*, Regina reflected.

The past cannot be changed but the future can. Regina realised then that forgiveness was not so much about what we receive from people but what we give them. Now she understood the anonymous quote: forgiveness is the scent that the rose leaves on the heel that crushes it.

Eventually they had a cinematic minute. Ma Hawa broke into tears, hugged Regina and said, 'My daughter, what I did was wicked. I once again ask for your forgiveness.'

'I forgave you mom.'

'I love you and am forever sorry.'

Regina's relationship with Ma Hawa changed dramatically after that détente minute. It became intimate, closer than it ever was.

ABOUT THE AUTHOR

Edward Aaron Mugabi is better known as a decentralisation and local development professional. He worked on programs in Liberia, Nigeria, Sierra Leone and his native Uganda. He always felt a calling to write. Now living quietly, he spends time fulfilling his passion of writing. **Thorns and Roses** is Edward's second novella. The first was **Dreams From The Soul.**

www.ingramcontent.com/pod-product-compliance
Lightning Source LLC
Chambersburg PA
CBHW061431160726
47995CB00003B/844